THIS BLOOMSBURY BOOK

BELONGS TO

Ròisìng Abbott

To my daughters, Sarah and Samantha – *PB*

To David, love Dad – *MT*

First published in Great Britain in 2004 by Bloomsbury Publishing Plc
36 Soho Square, London, W1D 3QY
This paperback edition first published in 2005
Text copyright © Peter Blight 2004
Illustrations copyright © Michael Terry 2004
The moral rights of the author and illustrator have been asserted

A CIP catalogue record of this book is available from the British Library

ISBN 0 7475 7144 9
ISBN-13: 9780747571445
Printed in China

10 9 8 7 6

All papers used by Bloomsbury Publishing are natural, recyclable products
made from wood grown in well-managed forests. The manufacturing
processes conform to the environmental regulations of the country of origin.

The Lonely Giraffe

by Peter Blight

illustrated by Michael Terry

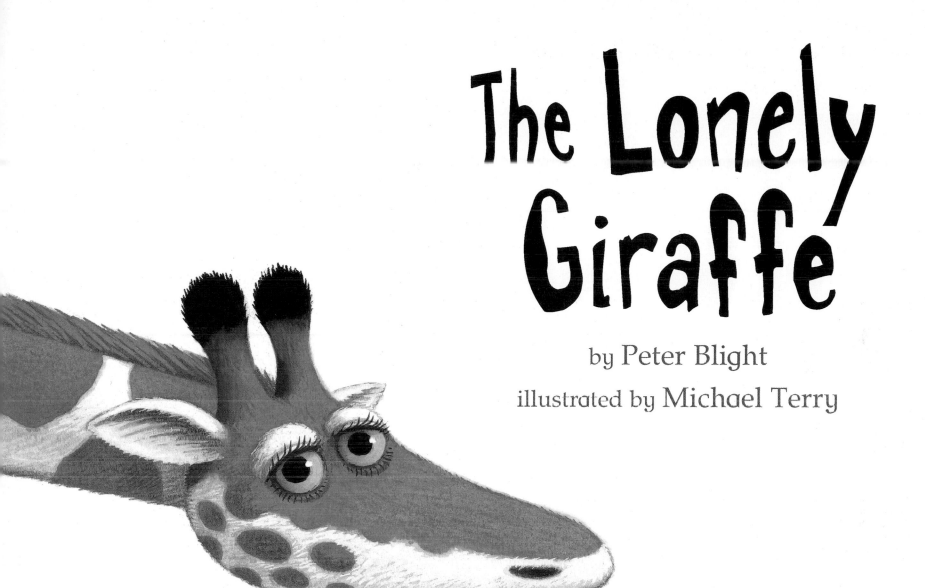

BLOOMSBURY
CHILDREN'S
BOOKS

The jungle animals were really quite a friendly bunch.
Every day the cockatoos were first to shake their feathers
and wake up the other animals.

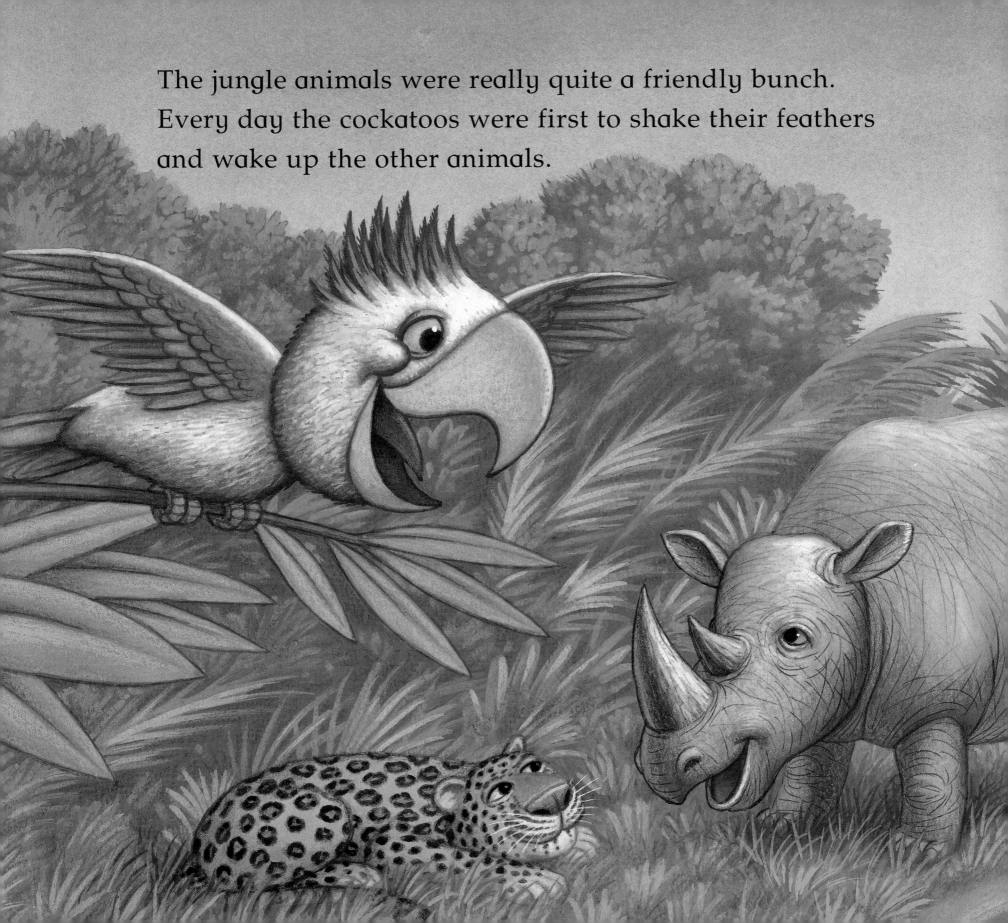

The elephants would trumpet "good morning"
and the snakes would hiss "hello".
Even the grumpy lion managed a friendly growl.

All the animals met near the river for breakfast every morning to discuss the jungle news. Everyone took their turn to speak, but no one listened to the giraffe.

The giraffe was just too tall. By the time he had spread his spindly legs and lowered his head to the ground the other animals had lost interest.

So the giraffe would lift his long neck and wander off.

He spent all day with his head in the trees eating the sweetest leaves.

He didn't realise that the birds and the monkeys that lived in the trees were frightened of his large head suddenly appearing in the treetops. Or that the small animals on the ground ran away because they were scared of being trodden on.

In the end the lonely giraffe didn't bother trying to speak to anyone. He moved from tree to tree munching on the leaves, and the jungle creatures went on avoiding him. That was how it went for the whole of the long dry summer.

When the rainy season came the large animals headed for the high ground. The small creatures sheltered in the bushes near the river, and the monkeys took cover in the trees. The rain poured down for days. The jungle animals became frightened that the river would burst its banks.

"Don't worry," said the alligator. "I'll carry you to safety in my big wide jaws!"

But the animals didn't trust him.

As the river rose the jungle creatures
became even more frightened.
They huddled together
beneath the bushes.

And no one heard the distant roar until the leopard pricked
up his ears. But nobody could think what it was.
  The giraffe looked over the heads of the animals
on the ground. His big eyes widened like saucers
and he slowly bent his spotted neck until the
worried creatures could hear him.

"The river is flooding," said the giraffe in a surprisingly squeaky voice. "A wall of water is racing down the valley."

"What can we do?" asked the gazelle. "It's too late to run away."

"We'll all be drowned," squeaked the mouse.

"Or the alligator will eat us," hissed the snake.

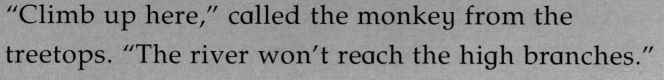

"Climb up here," called the monkey from the treetops. "The river won't reach the high branches."

"Hurry," squawked the cockatoo. "I can see the water coming."

The jungle animals raced to the trees. But some of them could not climb up the slippery tree trunks. Their hooves and tails were not made for climbing.

The roaring water rushed closer and the animals shivered with fright.

Then the giraffe had an idea. He bent his knees and spoke to the animals. "Climb on to my back," he squeaked in his high voice. "The water is almost here."

The river was lapping around the creatures. The monkey jumped up the giraffe's neck and called to the others. The hairy wart hog was next to carefully climb on.

One by one the animals helped each other to safety.

Then the giraffe straightened his knees
as the water flooded the jungle.

He stretched up his long neck and the
last few animals hurried into the branches,
helped by the chattering monkeys. The
water washed around the giraffe's strong
legs and sprayed the animals in the trees.

Then the river rushed on. The water slowly sank back to the ground and the sun came out from behind the clouds.

The giraffe poked his head up
into the high branches and
the animals slid down his
back to the damp earth.

From that day on the
giraffe was never lonely again.
The jungle animals would wait for the giraffe to lower his head
and join in the conversation. The birds and monkeys in the
trees were no longer afraid of the giraffe's big head. The
cockatoos would find the sweetest leaves for the brave
giraffe. The elephants would trumpet "good morning"
and the snakes would hiss "hello". And the grumpy lion
would pretend to growl before falling asleep in the sunshine.

Enjoy more fantastic picture books from the illustrator Michael Terry ...

Little Hotchpotch
Brian Patten & Michael Terry

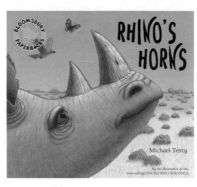

Rhino's Horns
Michael Terry

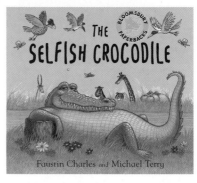

The Selfish Crocodile
Faustin Charles & Michael Terry

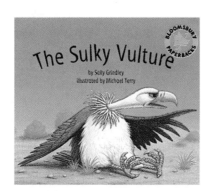

The Sulky Vulture
Sally Grindley & Michael Terry

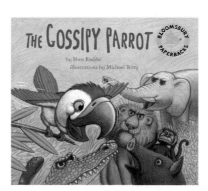

The Gossipy Parrot
Shen Roddie & Michael Terry

All now available in paperback